PEE-U-U-U-U!

PEE-U-U!

Please Don't Upset P.U. Zorilla!

LYNN Rowe Reed

Alfred A. Knopf   New York

THIS IS A BORZOI BOOK PUBLISHED BY ALFRED A. KNOPF

Published in the United States by Alfred A. Knopf, an imprint of Random House Children's Books, a division of Random House, Inc., New York.

KNOPF, BORZOI BOOKS, and the colophon are registered trademarks of Random House, Inc.

www.randomhouse.com/kids

Educators and librarians, for a variety of teaching tools, visit us at www.randomhouse.com/teachers

Library of Congress Cataloging-in-Publication Data
Reed, Lynn Rowe.
Please don't upset P.U. Zorilla! / Lynn Rowe Reed. — 1st ed.
    p. cm.
SUMMARY: After moving to a new town, a skunk has several mishaps before he finally finds a suitable job.
ISBN-13: 978-0-375-83654-1 (trade) — ISBN-13: 978-0-375-93654-8 (lib. bdg.)
ISBN-10: 0-375-83654-3 (trade) — ISBN-10: 0-375-93654-8 (lib. bdg.)
[1. Skunks—Fiction.] I. Title. II. Title: Please do not upset P.U. Zorilla!
PZ7.R25273Ple 2006   [E]—dc22   2005035623

MANUFACTURED IN CHINA

10 9 8 7 6 5 4 3 2 1

First Edition

To my sister Judy

Dear Mr. Mayor,
My home was replaced by a
shopping mall. I am looking for
a new home. I am kind, hardworking,
generally smell fine, and am good with
children and animals. May I come to
your town to live?

Sincerely,
P.U. Zorilla

. . . and he welcomed P.U. Zorilla with open arms.

Mayor Tootlebee gave P.U. a job driving the school bus.

The first day went perfectly.

But on the second day, a fight broke out at the back of the bus and spread all the way to the front.

All that arguing was making P.U. upset.

His tail began to lift . . . and lift. Suddenly a
gush of skunk spray sprang from his behind.
The kids were aghast.

office

Mayor Tootlebee took P.U. Zorilla to his office. "You are finished working around children," he scolded.

They drove to the pet store.

PETS

The mayor told its owner,
"He is kind and will
work hard for you.

But please..."

P.U. was good with the animals.

He loved the dogs and the cats
and the rabbits
and the gerbils . . .

. . . but not the snake!

PEE-U-U-U-U!

Mayor Tootlebee was determined to find the right job for P.U. He asked, "What is your most favorite thing?" "Baseball," replied P.U.

"Then you should sell popcorn at the baseball games," announced the mayor.

And he arranged for P.U. to sell popcorn that very night.

In the evening, Mayor Tootlebee took P.U. Zorilla to the ballpark. P.U. sold more popcorn during one game than anyone ever had before.

CORN

All was well until a
ball came flying from the
field and knocked P.U. Zorilla
on the noggin.

Mayor Tootlebee
shouted, "Please . . ."

"...don't upset P.U. Zorilla!"

But it was too late.

"Foul!" shouted the umpire.

FOUL, INDEED!

"You have one last chance," the mayor warned P.U. "Your job will be to clean my wife's store at night." The mayor took P.U. to Mrs. Tootlebee's store and left him with her.

JEWELRY

Before leaving, Mrs. Tootlebee
showed P.U. what to do.

As she turned to go, a big,
bad man in a ski mask hit
Mrs. Tootlebee over the head.

She was out cold!
Then he scooped up a bag
full of diamond rings
and necklaces.

P.U. Zorilla could only imagine how mad Mayor
Tootlebee would be if the store was robbed.

He turned to the robber and said, "PLEASE..."

"...DON'T UPSET P.U. ZORILLA!"

But it was too late. P.U. cracked—and I mean cracked—under pressure. First, the spray hit the robber in the face. He swayed and fell to the floor. Then the smell reached Mrs. Tootlebee's nose and awakened her.

Z·Z·Z·Z·Z

When the mayor and the police arrived,
Mrs. Tootlebee was hugging and kissing
her hero, P.U. Zorilla.

Mayor Tootlebee gave
P.U. a new job.

And he gave his town a new name.

WELCOME TO STINKVILLE
where smelling good isn't everything
Mayor: THOMAS TOOTLEBEE
Chief of Police: P.U. ZORILLA